"Listening. And then there's listening. Where you stop the mind and become all ears. Tonight there'll be a harvest moon, and then you'll separate the wheat from the crap. You wonder, autumn means what in Kenya, India, Malaysia? You know where you are, and what it's like here."

—NO-ONE'S-LAND
(FOUR POSTCARDS ON A THEME)

Sub-Rosa
&
Other Fiction

Catherine Bennett

ANVIL PRESS PUBLISHERS

Copyright © 1997 by Catherine Bennett

All rights reserved. No part of this book may be reproduced by any means without the prior written permission of the publisher, with the exception of brief passages in reviews. Any request for photocopying or other reprographic copying of any part of this book must be directed in writing to the Canadian Reprography Collective (CANCOPY), 6 Adelaide Street East, Suite 900, Toronto, Ontario, Canada, M5C 1H6.

This is a work of fiction. Resemblances to people
alive or dead are purely coincidental.

Cover design by JT Osborne

Printed and bound in Canada by Kromar Printing
First Edition

Canadian Cataloguing in Publication Data

Bennett, Catherine, 1958-
Sub-rosa & other fiction
ISBN 1-895636-11-6
I. Title
PS8553.E63S92 1996   C813'.54   C96-910382-4
PR9199.3.B3777S92 1996

Represented in Canada by the Literary Press Group
Distributed by General Distribution Services

Anvil Press
Suite 204A—175 East Broadway,
Vancouver, BC
Canada   V5T 1W2

ACKNOWLEDGEMENTS

Some of these pieces have appeared in slightly different form in *sub-TERRAIN, Grain, Tessera,* and in the chapbook *3Works* (Sprang Texts, 1992).

I wish to thank the Canada Council's Explorations Program for financial assistance during the writing of this book.

Several unacknowledged quotations appear in the text:

"Lines": *I want to say everything.* This was a much-discussed concept in writer/filmmaker Abigail Child's "Melodrama and Montage" seminar, given at the Kootenay School of Writing in August 1991.

"Strike Up the Dead": *You never love. You yourself never loved.* From *Dracula* by Bram Stoker; *Paths of flame. And there do her feet walk; Having thought of it, I must not dishonour it.* Adapted from *Dracula* by Bram Stoker; *Have I been dreaming.* From *Carmilla* by J. Sheridan Le Fanu.

"Jane Eyre, Revisited": *Absent from me...; longed for a power of vision...; Anybody may blame me who likes.* From *Jane Eyre* by Charlotte Brontë.

"Renée Vivien": *the infinite charm of desire and regret; They tortured me so unintentionally and so gracefully; The tobacco flowers...* From *A Woman Appeared to Me* by Renée Vivien; *Young women of the future society.* From the dedication to *The Song of Bilitis* by Pierre Loüys; *Being love's slave...* Adapted from William Shakespeare's Sonnet #57.

Thanks to Jennifer Glossop for her advice and encouragement.

I am particularly indebted to Colin Smith for his close reading of this manuscript, his suggestions, his friendship, and his patience.

Table of Contents

Safe to the Edge	9
Lines	13
They Look Different . . .	22
b & w	24
Strike Up the Dead	30
Jane Eyre, Revisited	37
Ficture Theory	40
French Horses	46
Loft	49
Mission	68
Renée Vivien	71
Four Postcards on a Theme	78
Music, Sweet & Cold	84
Shoes	91
Sub-Rosa	94
Whiskey Sour	98
Autobiography	106

SAFE TO THE EDGE
(an introduction for starters)

Solo beautiful
       damn
               and take it from the top. Always outmanoeuvred, but only just; we must never acknowledge it, so we let it fall. Why not? Without calling that pulse, it warbling hails. I always have my fingers at the ready. I remember now—it was much to do with wanting, distracted in the middle and safe to the edge. One first, so that there might be other; savoury and estranged and tumbling divinely. Fit to be sung, or spoken of, yet not yet. It is to do with not knowing, disunderstanding. High treason, fully committed to crimes. Old chapel hymns (which have their perplexities) say
               Don't
                             be
     so
                sure.

Draw back as if burned and for Christsake. Might we merely less of everything and please indeed no. It isn't always as it sometimes does, and please yourself. Learn a time, learn ungovernable wants how thin they become at the edges. Beautiful, friable. There could be voices rising in sleep, and rich mouths, a certain quality of listening that bears too much. They come posed as strange and loving animals, a fragmented, gentrified slow dance though nothing is quite so celestial. Old chapel hymns (which would be uplifting) ask

                        Who

                wants

       to know?

Just give a moment its character by going without a clue a bit longer. It be like that and bring it to be. Speak now *and* forever hold your peace, would that that would be worth the listening to. Think about laying eggs; they, after all, have wings indeed. Now. Patience for now: can you stand it.

    Hostile impeccable

                scarred

                            and heave it over the top. *Work for it, bitch, nothing comes easy* so no lieback at once. But the ardent beasts are as I left them last night and just the way I want them. How splendid, how fortuitous, how precipitously manipulative. Ecstasy sports a religious language. Either/or become neutral and better off for it, though they may write us from time to time. Where eggs and choirmasters plummet. That wanting is quite a desire. After a fashion, all answers, how dare you, are custom.

It isn't always as it sometimes dares; still, I would argue, and warble. Ungovernable wants bear us to and from sleep; it is what we do instead of mortgages. For its own sake; all of a madness. How to know when a time is fit I wish I could, but those eras are broken to avoid equanimable sequence. As is. Not yet. That kind of want can take the place, and verve its own deferment. Fingers are never quick enough for that.

A kind of religion can take the place. The ardent beasts in deferment know a protracted excitement; they will arrive solely and at once. But not yet. And thus become contemplatives. At the edge, sleep, dreams, all husks, are monastic, are ecstatic without effort. To do with wanting, and going without a bit longer. Beyond the edge we know not what, but if eggs can fly let us slide over.

Prayer
moderate

strung and rising to the top *or sing instead, voices are like that.* One following another past the edge, none stopping to think. In fact, it is dark out there but we should have expected and the pulse is full of endearments. Beast or no, it is an amorous brooding, and something to think about as love's rats heave to. What to take with us as we flow to know not what, we expected or assumed. We were warned: it was chancy but do we listen? But to the lulling endearments, form a gorgeous narcotic and so. Prayer goes where, and there we are. Sang over the top, I did, I heard; naughty, lovely, gentle thing.

Sequence in music: that repeated in another key, or a

second chance to die for. Words, and the sounds they propose. The unconveyable—there is process, forbearance; not once again but yet again. Where sound would be, surpassing yet again to loop its own delight, altered and inflected. Given one's druthers, why not again, but different this time and eccentric to itself and becoming some other? Though old chapel hymns (which get contumacious) may simply say
    Play
   it
     again.

Write me backwards and maybe I'll understand, or sift such music to the wind. It wiles and trills and anyway. Rebound, comes once another tender beast, all warm nostrils and heavy scent. Eminent. Credible. Retreat may be sounded, but not necessarily frantically obeyed. At the centre: safe, sure, but we never know just what that is. Where we are, yet the beasts arrive. On the other, the drop could take longer than we have left. We could call it home. Old chapel hymns (full of lovely palaver) say
    Send
     a
      postcard.

LINES

To me from the scent of him, drifting low through cigarettes and sweat, not ours, the congress of beer and saliva. Want to know his hands on her skin whichever way they kiss. I respect details, not privacy, want flesh layered to the dream.

Kissed me once in the hallway of a party. All her in the throttle of this dream blow-out. She did that. One kiss. Two mouths, four lips, physical components squared to the nth degree. Now it's this night again and she has a hand in me almost like we'd never done it before. She came from him sometime before and I knew about doing this even when they were. Her shirt not just off her shoulders, strip of skin between buttons and holes. She knelt over me we had the complex to condense our cravings on. He wasn't with us. I have always wanted lines to cross.

Sometimes at the deepest point with her I want to count. One, two, three . . . Waves. I roll onto my elbow for a different angle. She looks like a photograph like this, but she moves. Between the two of us. She and I alone have breasts, we have skin, we have the palms of our hands, I have legs that can't grip her strong enough. There is a certain quality of air among us. I know there will be years when I'll remember this. Posture of her head, and her lipsticked, dark lower lip.

At a party with night falling fast through the window. Each face an attitude, a thought: many the personae, few the people. I wanted to lose expectant detail. An old broad armchair was moved into the kitchen, and I sat, testing the brocade with my fingers. Texture. I sat in its lap and she perched on its arm; though her head was turned away from me, she wasn't talking to me, I liked the way her legs looked reaching to the floor, anticipation of her feet that would before long move away from me. The shadow cast by her jaw on her chest, throwing one whole shoulder into darkness.

She was in this city, temporarily from hers. I left the armchair first.

In the living-room he wandered, beer bottle in hand, in dread of what he wanted. His face not an attitude. Couldn't stand it. I wanted to dance with him, slung my arm around his shoulders and danced with him hip to hip, brother my rival. He was hard under my arm but we moved together, and Queen Latifah's voice, loud and hot from the speakers, sang that ladies must come first. Yet. When it was time to go it was clear she'd leave with him but she stopped me in the hallway and put her lips to my throat and bit. Then the side of my face. Then mouth to mouth. Swear I could taste it. We are not mathematicians, but we know how to multiply. She was leaving with him, he was happy, light-headed; and I had kissed the air he walked on.

Some element of me vital in their coming together.

Infinitive of the word "conspiracy": to be a party to. I have always wanted lines to cross.

I want to know everything. I have involved myself yet and again. She came to me for a first night but it was still from him, it was always from him. Could smell him, rocking with my breath as soon as she came near me. She said "He gave me a book. He said too much gets lost between line and line, that we are never enough. He told me we are fucking each other over, and go and start it with her I don't care about it. Just don't say anything to me. Please." At some point that night my hand intercepted the path left by his on her skin, but she was the motional one, making tracks for both of us. We do not petition forgetfulness.

Afterwards, exhausted together in the café. So bright we stared at our own reflections in the darkened glass windows, transparent and ghostly. Espresso made no impression on my tempered body. She had taken time to bind up her hair in a striped scarf, but she was still breathing through parted lips. Who did I look at sitting across from me, gypsy, sex partner, habitué. What I wanted was the continual unfolding, her jawline in one angle begging to differ in another light, her eyes deflecting café lamp-shine. The mode of her body foliated with dreams indicating a way: we can be not who we are, or have ever thought. I can wrench you out of your who.

She does not petition forgetfulness in the shape of an encounter. I think the path of my intention as twisted as the scarf
> holding back
her extravagant hair.

Her perpetual line: "We can do it another way."

All day long I thought of her, and what he had in her. Brother my rival. Wrapped with her in a bed or mattress on the floor, he is cash poor and bereft of property, the more purely to come to her. She wouldn't want to see him after leaving me she flew between us like word of mouth. Sometimes no sex with him. They walked together through the dark and cold, on the cheap and on the sly. I am comfortable at home in my downtown apartment, complicit and humiliated a thousand ways, more than words will tell.

I want to say everything. I'm fucking him too though I swear I've never touched him, I have never put my finger to his mouth or gone into him with a knuckle, a finger, a fist, but I know more about lubricants than is good for a human being. He is not with us, but he's always there, I can at all times hear him breathing. And I connive at times, this no sex with him, compulsive, obsessive, manic depressive, shotgun of sex never far from our collective heads. I think some of his thoughts. I fathom her too but only with him. Just to know all about it. Harm's way. I keep a journal describing every sexual encounter, real or not. Mine or not. I call the journal *Harm's Way*.

I have identified the taste I desire as salt. All day long I thought of her. She may have bit me the first time she kissed me. I call up his face the way it was at the party, interminably touching. I would like to dance with him, join with him once again, but now it is she and he who are hip to hip. His face seemed to talk simultaneously about staying and leaving, how you sometimes get what you want. Dread. At night, I have plunging and vicious dreams.

In the café she asked "Point out the woman you find most attractive," but we had just had sex and I was looking at her. Then I indicated the one I thought *she* would find most attractive.

We are fucking each other over.

In harm's way we are fucking each other over. Incessant. Every kiss they share splits me open wider and more desperate. I tumult and pitch myself to her wiser graces. Shed analysis, annul method. I am at the height of my persistent who, and I want the long terrible pleasure of falling.

~ 17 ~

Years when I'll remember this. I'll know. It will be the last look I have of her and her hair was down from the scarf, she seemed newly created. Her gaze locked with my eyes, she kept and kept on doing it. She said, "more than ever."

She quickens herself between city and city. She says "One really needs so little." She knows so little of the life I lead, the regular, insatiable grind.

> **excerpt**
> . . . *swollen and bruised w/sex, her face my face looks consumed in our common looking-glass. We smoked dope last night, she put the live end of the joint in her mouth & waited till the smoke had collected under her palate then put her lips against mine & filled me w/a jet of hot & bitter narcotic smoke. Eating fire. Haze after that. She put her head against my breast or bone, rolled her head across my chest her hair trailing after. Skin aqueous, lucid & membrane. She lies on top of me till the world of day jobs & rent money falls away, simmers into me & draws him in w/her. This time, this dream I look from my own body with unaccustomed eyes.*

Things get complex. The body is foliated with vicious dreams. We are never enough. I would warp myself infinitely, would eat the lives of others if I had the power. And then have all at once. I bide my time. Sometimes after sex, at 2 or 3 A.M. we have to get out of bed and walk just to know we have legs, just to know we are other than one ecstatic flesh. On her body I experience her speed, impeccable and terrified. She speaks without talking, says I can wrench you out of your who. Buttons and holes. When I can and when I can stand it, I look into her eyes, hold my breath and travel deep until I founder on what I think is his reflection. In the jungled and deep opium breath of sex I blessed and obliterated can question who I am. I bide my time.

His reflection of the situation is don't say. If he thinks nothing he can take peace. With peace he can feel anything. He is a couple, not one of three when she disappears at night, he can tell himself whatever. It doesn't work, the pieces all spin out. He is there in spite of himself. I want to own his intentions too.

> ***excerpt***
> *. . . who she is tonight. I'm on all fours w/her body under mine, looking down @ her, twisting my head into every angle to look @ her in all possible ways, till I find an angle that makes her face look a shade somewhat. Like his. Start kissing her, lip to lip. Can't stop. Lip trespasses lip. Teeth. Taste salt.*

I want to undo the expectant detail. I want to be undone of everything. I want the dread of what I want, the continual unfolding. Each angle turning on itself to create a new picture, every picture shifting and changing its light.

I could learn ascension on the flat of her back. I could

be merciful and swift and glutted with luxury. Coming to it quickly now or some certain possibility. All three of us working the each of the other.

> **excerpt**
> *. . . this afternoon, going down on her yet attuned to her climbing voice. My head buried in texture, the exquisite slippage of her skin but she must have been w/him earlier in the day because I know what I found between her legs. Bodies without boundaries. I am so close to having it all. Her legs spread & my who opened wider than it ever nightmared. Treasured quality of dread. Lost track of the times she came I came I have always wanted lines to cross.*

I imagine a letter that I'll write to her. The letter will say ". . . would do it, would drop everything just to fuck you over . . . ."

I have always longed for perpetual motion, the dedication to thought submerged in purpose. I have long admired desperate measures. I take my comfort in transition, the verge of forever becoming. We keep it becoming. Thinking of her, he hears my name. I imagine her eyes and see his reflection. I live in a state of prodigious dimensions, our lives layered together, compressed or poisoned it never mattered. When she surpasses she draws me up with her. No matter where I am I have the pleasure of falling.

Texture is what I rub my skin against, the grain and slip of contact, what I most dread, where the worst abrasions can occur. Fingers to the brocade. If I am hurt, it is not in any accepted way. Desperate measures. How we twine to each other, swollen and bruised desperate measures no matter what.

My fall begins with the pit of the stomach. This one comes through layers of skin and tissue, smoke scent (not ours) and taste salt. Strata. Layers of skin (don't know whose), a brilliant intractable dream. Losing it, prodigal and singular, roaring out the pinnacle.

There will come that moment. We are sitting in the café. Her hair is down from her scarf. She is saying the phrase "more than ever."

I am "more than ever." I keep on and on.

THEY LOOK DIFFERENT BECAUSE THEY'VE THOUGHT ABOUT IT

Not just for the watching, and staying present. Why else would I come? All I wanted to do was kiss, really. My hand flashed up, my little finger got locked in someone's tit ring. Stepitup. Her feet pumping down the boardwalk. They look different here because they've had to think about it. My finger as if married to that hoop of gold, if I'd pulled then there would have been blood everywhere.

Rape is always a possibility. Some people don't like us when we leave. Under T-shirts, oiled with sweat. Between flashing lights I watched them kiss; like tasting the lips of nuns. In the park she jogs alone. I said, "That's dangerous." Just this afternoon I was outside, and I can't believe.

Into it. The way I move here you'd think I never had a day job. For those twenty minutes between here and my place my heart pounds fastandheavy all the way.

When it's tough to breathe she moistens her lips with peach schnapps. Between watch and dance I can't decide. Wild by desire, but could never call myself a slamster, plotting a course home through light, through people, through alcohol antiseptic. When attacked, can I throw the bottle? Can't take it with you from the only place you could see a kiss like that.

They look different here because they've thought about it. Eight miles a day down the boardwalk she got those muscles. Under pressure. She put her tit ring away under her T-shirt, you wouldn't believe anything unusual. They all have hair that makes hands desire. My mouth swims through peach schnapps to where the skin of her lips begins or anyhow, thinking about it. One more hoop of gold moved from injury's way. Touching lips the way nuns kiss before the chancing walk home. I said, "That's dangerous."

b&w

Darkened backgrounds and certain faces. These are props—well enough. But catalyst is the contemplation of expression. Eyes, and contours of lip. And look: the expression may be something of mine; but what a mad solecism—of what is she thinking? The setting might be *fin de siècle*, and the skin Victorian. Black and white has all the makings of fantasy: it is ether, history and fallacy in sensory material. For questionable motives, it must be choice.

The method of approaching the lens is called *mien*. *Look*. And *look out*. Unless the eyes are very light, this process will make them completely dark. Gaze, as can be said, has more to do with desire than expression. *Lies indeed*. The reflective suggestion of dilated pupils—they open up, and they remain a cloistered dark. Just before the flash. Upon looking closer, and closer, we discover a trail: the mocking hunt.

Pose:
 "white silk with dark wood chair"
 standing, her hand resting on the back of the chair, one knee resting on the seat.
  she takes to polished wood as if she owns it.
 more skin than silk, ah! she is very pale.
  triumphant. incongruous.
 her face turned away and looking distant—without the glance we cannot know.
 she may know her mind. for whom was she taken?

Gloss over matte—the glamour, of course, and it's icy to fix upon. It is choice. To remain unsmudged, the photographs are plucked by their edges: too fragile and incipiently culpable. Having something to tell, they opt for a chemical layer, the high sheen of meddlement. They play their part—being pleasing and interfering at a single blow.

Sepia might be gentler than black and white, but no more rewarding; conveying by degrees, abandoned in another era. It, too, expresses by abstraction, leaving conception as a sweeter process. Fancy this: that the silk might be ivory, the wood deep reddish brown. And still in the mind the picture does not harshen. Stealth and cunning, evasion of colouration, with barely a hint of defiance. We are being managed, conceivably, but we are too deep in the matter: if only for the sake of discretion, we should stop looking now.

> *Pose:*
> *"the red shirt"*
> *but a dark shade of grey and such fine weave to fall so engagingly. her back faces the camera,*
> *her face a profile and composed. in her present mood, she spurs restraint. those pleasing shoulders evade the fabric. a woman stepping into her bath? or bed.*
> *the garment very here and now and her expression so demure.*
> *she must have found that out of sometime. without the gaze, what do we know?*
> *her back is very beautiful.*

And where, for the life of us, might we be now? Perhaps this is a temple? We partake of her so wholly and without fulfilment. It was years ago; I no longer know who she is; I see her everywhere. I cannot cease looking. We are in mocking hunt: open the album, and she is sure to be there.

Her postures are vestal, and praise the ostentation of her skin. We should not mistake it for anything else, but how can we avoid enjoying what it is? Anachronism. Did no one tell her of her own time and its blatant looks? The photos were taken, it is strange and all for what. *Nonnette, my nonnette, why display the body and shy the face?* Cautious, nonetheless, we do not wish to breach her protocol.

The sight of that skin is a deep and blasted satisfaction. It is choice. She would not pretend to be unobserved, and we have been told: it is rude to stare.

Black and white, and pose. The makings of fantasy are unornamented at that, but set them on to each other and we will provoke something much out of hand. We have not simply looked; we have "processed." Questionable motives, abstraction, conception—these are fine words, assuredly. We shall keep them close by, for we may have need of them.

She carries her awareness with fetching style. She relished the focus on her back as she slipped her shirt from those shoulders and arrested its fall just above her hips. As she turned her face to partial darkness. Of what could she have been thinking? *Mien.* These poses were perhaps self-preservation. *Ah.* That self. Ah. Yes. What is being done to us? I, for one, have for some time longed to sway to the inducement of her dilated pupils.

As if we don't love near-perfection and mystery. It develops our capacity to look. It makes us want to fumble for those close-by words, of photos and telling; how all the little flaws disappear in that process. We love it for that, for so many reasons.

Be that as it may, the expression is still something of mine. But without the look in her eyes, how shall I say? She was very cunning: the darkened background, the black velvet drop, would make her stand out all the more.

Pose:
"over the shoulder, eyes down"
*   hah! she is on guard!*
* but subtle. her back again and blazing white.*
*   her face—almost!*
turned toward the shoulder,
*   the shoulder stilled in the act*
of turning to the camera. if but for her eyes.
*   just if simply, if only if.*
*   altogether so much light.*

For the sake of discretion, I should say nothing. This third is my favourite. Provoking out of hand, something here smacks of radiance. Rife in promise and so withholding, abandoned in another era. Then, and now. Black, and white, and pose. Elements in the mocking hunt.

What a collection. Pictures so she can be both more and different than she is. There is something always almost telling, the sly tilt of her shoulders throughout. I have seen her everywhere indeed: on sidewalks, in shop windows and reflective surfaces, but always I miss the expanded pupils. And these are such photographs as any can see.

More than can be contained in any one image or style or time. *Fin de siècle?* Or only too blatant? We are spared the disaster of being certain. Her looks are privacies, they travel somewhere still. In future, I think, she will peruse this collection with inexhaustible curiosity.

Meddlement in a word; it is rude to stare; still, it is

something of mine. *Shy the face, and get them thinking.* We could justify for what we draw upon her: questionable motives, abstraction, conception—this process may make them completely dark. She opts for black and white, shades of grey, and blazing light across her back. Without colour, left to our own devices; it is what she wanted. We love it for that.

For so many reasons.

Black velvet backdrop. Or so it looks from here.

Pose:
"the collection"

            over time.
    we have her by the edges.

            blatant.
blasted.
    no colour at all,
      altogether so much longing.
   how can we avoid enjoying what it is?

STRIKE UP THE DEAD
(a vampire tale)

*I seemed somehow to know her face, and to know it in
connection with some dreamy fear . . .*
Bram Stoker, *Dracula*

*"I was all but assassinated
in my bed, wounded here . . . and never was
the same since."*
J. Sheridan Le Fanu, *Carmilla*

She did appear that sleep as it comes, loaded and waiting, rich by abduction. By time the way it furls. That we can be led on; eyes closed. Eyes snuffed. Dimness that doesn't quite. Comes baled with those images, raising one hand, deposit of gesture, slipping, drifting, knowing what comes next. Going under. One finger raised, but who's counting.

Am I cold? Have I given out. What more could I obliterate for? To burn in hell forever, drawing off, or drawing on apace, an antique manner to say. Unfurling. Giving up. That was a different century, her dark heavy paths. That was her stride I heard last night whispering "inside inside inside." The dire fabric. And I in something red with a low neckline; with her ever on this one.

The possibility of danger. Yes. That does mean something. A space for reckoning, a space for quiet.

This is a grave suspicion: there is everything to say for it. Not said in one century and must not in another. I am becalmed with a peculiar ardour, to find myself at these devices. Having thought of it, I must not dishonour it. On those paths is my tongue stopped. Given the task how can I, peculiar, aspire? Paths of flame. And there do her feet walk. A grave suspicion, one cannot proceed too quickly; one must, of necessity, go cautiously. With faith, and savour.

As it moves, now and ever. In sleep and recall: a face pressed to mine. Coldly pressed. A face much at once beheld and beloved. Diligent, always, and put to memory in procuring the details; but hair, her flaxen hair, silver in the moonlight: that colour that men not known for anything else have been known to die for. Her mouth with its stolen goods and a forehead for the ages. Placed all together and still no telling, baled with those images. So throat, so skin. Such apprehension, achieved in diverse passages. There is myself, in sickness or other, in parcel of flesh, state of mind. Temporarily stateless. Sleeping, the way I did come upon this ground.

Of why. This particular ground. The most innocent

reason; I know mine worse than anybody. None can ever get enough of raising the stakes.

Loaded and waiting, what opening to nineteenth-century wisdom. I wouldn't remember if I didn't want it. Given over, indolently. To long for, and cede. To come again, coldly pressed beneath her dark and heavy skirts. She is a woman with a mouth, her mouth, the way I've been used.

It's no use. My splintered thinking. I cannot account for myself.

What might she promise, of so few words and profuse suggestion? Striking such an acquaintance, what should I say, well met and full of surprises. What hasn't she heard before, all in all as if it mattered. What lips would one find such a time talking, to think of what could hear. How low a voice must be kept? At such a time. For such could it be, seemly and right, were it not for a most questionable spirit.

As it moves, so do I.

Thinking: replete. Satiety. Glutted. Or any of the thousand names of satisfaction. That graceful list. Stolen goods. Worth having; worth fearing. Something enters this way, a dream of fear. A double embrace, participant and vessel, the dream of her face. Floating near the surface of memory, not quite anchored. Swift and unsettled.

May I say that peculiar ardour of mine, so draining, so

extraordinarily grieved and satisfying, the scantest veneer through which bevels everything. I should not to anyone, not in one century or must not another. What an egress am I, drawing off and taking myself with me; this is not unpleasant. I would not have it thought that this is unpleasant.

You never love. I have heard those words before. *You yourself never loved.* So I stand, with these words telling. Her voice, so near my own throat. Surely I have heard this before. How I stand, eyes snuffed, that voice vibrating the skin of my throat. From beyond rejoinder and past sense. Something to be taken up when I come for it. Moving off, down to a range of deeper sleep.

    The warmest drifts. The quiet tide. To sink like that: wounded here, so slowly, and with such great pleasure. Ambition, diversion, strongly and wholly replete with coma. This being the ingress: and so am I taken.

It is true that I have kept for myself. Coming in the night like that: how can she be trusted? Why this here looks soft what fine a resting place. Such admissions as I have. Her hair. I have yes known. Such face and skin for dusty memory. Her circled waist her looks soft the coldly pressed and dark and heavy skirts. Gathered from whirling dust and moonlight, the method of those who would. Drawn on so, they are discrete elements but flooding together; I cannot say. Have I done this before? I am known for anything else, such admissions as I have. Such a spurned and trifled offering, what would she take. Admissions, or whatever bows the head. Or sends it falling back, the throat swelling above the dire fabric.

I am cold. I have never loved. I am in these situations and confound my history. Examining my conscience I have found, tripped thick through catechisms praying, crying, for more. And what have I looked over my shoulder. Dainty vices and full-blooded coming: worth loving, worth fearing. Listen to this, and sorcery. With an ear full, an eye snuffed, a conscience at fault. A most questionable spirit. I should give it up if given the chance.

Symbols and trappings beside the dust and memory. These are found things. I think on them, their hardness of prayer. Less and less it matters, I am suspected. Maybe come the great soft tides once I that held to heart. What do they seem that I had? At such a loss, I would give all too much.

That does mean something. A space for reckoning; exactly. This one, and so. I cannot atone for myself.

Curious ardour: its latent demands, how familiar it seems. The discipline. The schooling of my earliest days to this, or something like this. I have perhaps got it wrong. Shuttered thought. For what feels right, may it be right, but was I never told. I have a grave what to go on. My ardour, exhausted, lies upon a strange bed from which it cannot rise. Nor will it rise. Stricken, it moves a most peculiar rest.

Borne on this, the quality of sleep. A secret, personal thing, an uncurled limb or racking back to the past; which past that plumbed her kind. Over now, and out of this she comes: the only way to stop her is through the heart. But this is too familiar.

Wherefore an offering, and say what kind. That ritual, I believe, could make important. Which one, could say, really needs? What kind ways her obliging; her teeth. The obligations of her teeth.

Say what I am now in the grip of. Have I been dreaming, whirring and throbbing that sleep as it comes. Thus loaded and waiting; my conscience desperately at fault. I have yes known. This is the dream where I hold my head a little strangely, making offer of my own throat. I could not accomplish awake. Loving as she can love, as I myself have never loved. On nineteenth-century terms. Scared to death and mad for it, in her arms the dead of night. Rendering account disallowed in my own time, full blooded, heavy scented, most wilfully, stubbornly given. So few things worth tossing back my head for, and yet this is one.

Knowing her face in dreamy fear, not given up nor set aside on any account. I would have spoken just so had I lived at the time, had I lived and kept account. I would state for the record: just so. Those who come after will be left to make of this.

But what, then, of the low neckline? So much will be made of that.

Too familiar that I should weaken, that I am troubled through my heart. In this alone my ardour stands me company, stricken though we are, each to its custom. Faith and savour, yet another list. Perhaps paths of flame, I am troubled, by my schooling perhaps. That we can be led on. And what should I return to apart from dust and memory? I had desires yes for somewhat beyond; for that have I given up my stake. For a mouth that vibrates the skin of my throat.

Say now once for me again what I am in the grip of. Admissions of existence. A swelling throat. A foundered conscience, or merely something red. I come for it, and would own it, or mad for it. Quarter and mercy am I taken, the trappings within the dust and memory. For what conscience have they their knowledge forged? Such profuse unspoken promise from one century to another, and that suggestion ever at her lips. The dream of her face, most grave and familiar.

JANE EYRE, REVISITED

I couldn't keep it straight in my mind: who was touching me? Jane or Rochester? "Absent from me and forgetting me quite, I'll be sworn," he said, but it was Jane's small hand that caressed my back. With Rochester, it would be easy, it was already scripted, but with Jane I would dare much. I would have to, we'd make it up as we went along.

That caressing hand. Its boldness surprised me, delighted me. It did cross my mind that it might be Rochester's; after all, he was lord of the manor. But no, Jane was there, making her presence felt. She was a governess, and had an authority of her own to be reckoned with.

I had read the book late in the night, for the twelfth time, and said to myself, "I know this book inside out." Then I was inside, and out was a matter of perspective. I had "longed for a power of vision which might overpass that limit"; now I had the midst of it. What kind of fiction was this? If we stayed with Rochester things would be fine, but if it was to be girl gets girl we'd have to write something new. Then wait for another century in which to publish it, because the early Victorians could be counted on not to understand. Rochester would never forgive me for taking Jane from him. And Charlotte Brontë already had scandal enough on her hands.

Because it was late, I'd said good night to Rochester, leaving him in the parlour with his brandy. I ran up the massive staircase, admiring in some part of my mind the dark lush wood of the balustrade. Hurrying along the gallery to Jane's room. Once safely inside with her I bolted the door, as Mrs. Rochester (the 1st) was known to escape from the top storey and bring her lunacy down into the house, where she once tried to burn Rochester in his bed. I stood shivering with cold, moonlight coming in through a crack in the heavy velvet curtains. A boundary had broken down somewhere; I'd slipped through and things were possible now, though just what would take some exploring. I wondered how to account for myself.

Does anyone know which way she'll use her tongue when the moment comes?

I looked to Jane, who was sitting up in bed, loosening the drawstring of her nightgown. "Once the madwoman upstairs gets loose," she said, "one never knows what may happen."

Much, much later, after the moon had set, I tried to steal away quietly from Jane's room, but stumbled across the doorjamb in the dark. As I tripped out into the hall, I found Rochester's arms around me, my head against his chest. Though it was uncalled for, it was not unpleasant.

Still, I've got some choices to make, and Jane's got the upper hand. Between her and Rochester, there's more territory than can be covered over one night in a coach and six. I'm taking my time. I'll be out when I'm ready.

"Anybody may blame me who likes."

FICTURE THEORY

But still don't I love you in your second language, perhaps, a slight misunderstanding. The accent here: my embarrassing weakness for women who speak French. So then; an imagined call/response, lust/regard, tell and lie. Split in two, or more. From the beginning, we could have talked preferences and thwarted agreements. The evening was a kind of chance, was it not? Though there were others present. Another scenario to plan for. Beach. Bar. What is the name for it. A trifling path, this (haven't I told you), put your lips there. In the presence of witnesses, nothing can happen. Therefore, this: *un peu méchant*. Without asking. Without leave.

Nothing can happen; that is an old story.

Put your lips here, yes, a stunning second language, together or apart. Those other two, ours, erstwhile estimable companions, drifting off. We end together in a bar with a view, my impossible hopes and so on. Do they call that "azure" do they call that "shining"; there should be a name for it. The beach at dusk. The presence of witnesses. Those other two staying on (reality), but in a second language something becomes. I keep your words while you order *"une autre martini,"* and those other two play suit. *Bien sûr. Belle sœur.* I lay all night with your head between my breasts but that was something else, a small surprise. A slight misunderstanding. In my way we are out on that beach, slipping, saying things we can't imagine. In the idiom. I love it, you bet, the profile, your pointed shoes, the slow voice. Speaking and timely; and that a merry dilemma.

Now then. Reconnoitre. My second language, which I don't speak. I am never in one place at a time; how to know where we're going. It just didn't sound like this when I thought about it. When we speak of what might have been as if it really was, we become quite interesting. *Belle sœur,* to talk like that. With a lip like yours, such humiliating envy. Now we become engaging, and how. I wouldn't say this to just anyone, I want you to know that, out there on that beach where my hand touched your face and I could feel the sand sinking, the sun finishing. It was almost complete at that point but *"une autre martini."* Full stop. So carelessly are we belayed. To make time with you, I'd have to start thinking about theory, about fiction; I was lost, indeed I was: lost from the moment I heard you.

Lost from the moment. If a woman says nothing in a bar, is she really there? Such humiliating envy.

Bien sûr, belle sœur. Once again your profile, the shoes, your slipping hair to make frustration concrete. How to get us from that bar to beach or my own bed (your head between my breasts, all night). To give those other two the slip would escape the presence of witnesses; just imagine. That might become. Therefore I would say unto those two: plead early mornings, late lovers, domestic duties if you must. But for, but for. Lovers in my own mind, unwatched I could make my fortune. I would say unto those other two, What a story I could tell, and you (two) are pre-empting it.

And such they are. My dalliance with your second language reduced to rubbing shoulders as we share the same side of the table. Our feet in the darkness beneath, only inches away from each other.

But still (as you may guess) this is the stuff upon which I build worlds.

Lovers in my own mind. *Belle sœur,* what to call you? No matter what name I use, those who know us will still say we were meant, and why should I want to make more liars in the world? Let them eat cake, for I have always loved the grand gesture. Let's say it happened: I swept you off your feet (from that darkness under the table); we found our feet on that dusky beach and my hands were on your shoulders. We experienced the most profound liplock woman has ever known. We were unnoticed, unwitnessed, and it was with such certainty I could hardly believe my luck. Myself . . .

Start over.

A woman says nothing in a bar and she is not really there, so I said "Have another drink." Present in the moment, I could stay that way if I could keep the words coming. Would you like to hear my definition of ecstasy? It's a prelude to something I haven't finished imagining. I have written sometimes about violent low-down dirty sex; there is that possibility, no? What is meant? In a second language, something goes on besides; how to know what we're really saying. Your slow-moving voice. I dream of hearing it while I'm half asleep, it seems as if I do. This morning for instance. "Have another drink."

Belle sœur, tu sais, sometimes that's the best way. Sense (as such) is not required. Therefore waking with your head between my breasts, thus a heavy weight, and ardently palpable. It must have happened, must it not? Something I haven't finished imagining: the heat of your skin on mine and the pressure of one slow grinding thigh. There is sand in my sheets. We were on the beach and you were saying yes or *oui* or yes or *oui* or alright or . . . "oh o.k."

Start over.

When I thought about it, it allowed me to lose my way for hours. A grand gesture. In my way, something becomes, but not often voiced. Perhaps in a second language the difference happens. But for the talk of those other two (erstwhile companions), so elegant and so full of theory we might have progressed. Ardent bed. Ardent beach. Shall I be reviled for preferring any woman to Wittgenstein?

Sometimes I think a kiss exists even before it reaches the destined lips—that is a theory. The presence of witnesses verifies what I couldn't make happen, and there should be a name for that. In the idiom. At such times I keep in mind suspension, all kinds, but find myself hovering about half an inch from your body. To make frustration concrete, and even the olive in your martini a picture of desire.

I like to imagine a second language accommodates what can't be said in this one. *Belle sœur,* tell me, is it like that? I like to imagine. Hovering, the theory, the kiss, and what I would be my sweet grand gesture. Without leave, for what it's worth, I was highly entertained by the thought of that beach, not a hundred yards from where we sat. Forever (or all evening) my mind mocked toward it, carrying an idea of you. And what a liplock: could we stay like that all night. I could, in theory, hovering that half-inch from your body.

Have another drink. Those fateful words. *Belle sœur,* what were you hearing? All, the suspension, the movement of my feet, my breath, and my lust for your martini's olive? All, or nothing much. Those words may be an invitation; yes we are aware, would you like to hear my definition of ecstasy? The exact moment at which your lips closed around the olive. I was sure (was I not?) I could not recover.

. . . "oh, o.k."

An existence, yes, lost from the moment but simultaneously in the translation. A treacherous dimension. In the same morning when I heard your voice and felt the weight of your head. That bruised pulpy feeling that comes only from a night of sex or from passing through *la turnstile sans mercy.* What had I done? *Belle sœur,* are you with me? What could become this flight of fancy? My second language (which I don't speak) seems to be this native tongue but what could be the name for it. Mercy is a premium, and how becoming. I have heard it said.

That is an old story. Beautiful sister. Very well. Separate in the presence of witnesses still something happened; but what and what? What that came from a long way off—I am still unsettled. Knowing it is half my work. Knowing it still, or moving, my impossible hopes and so on. Perhaps it didn't happen, doesn't mean, and still a stunning second language.

Belle sœur, I wanted you perhaps, but it is not as simple as that. Therefore this.

Which I build worlds.

FRENCH HORSES

Suggestion of speed and sexual activity, but nothing here stop looking. Why leap this now? Once I had a sorrel mare, but her leg and over. That speed. That think where devils me still. French horses.

French horses. They have a special style. They know particular things, possess exquisite instincts. They have a certain *je ne sais quoi*. I reason this, the flash of tail. It whips, stop looking. Sorrel such a strange colour because I could not find it. A horsing colour, yet another colour. What now to seek and be blamed for.

There it was, within her hide. A trancing thing. I spoke not her language nor she mine and it meant not. Their language of call and head toss. We run. I think myself onto her back, I think myself down to her hoof prints their inverted U. And the dust kick up your heels.

Equus is gone, so equestrienne. That feminine. She moved within her hide, see feel it. Some nights those hooves come pounding my sleep. Why now. By what means broken to it; I thought that mine but the saddle rocking with the arc of her back and her head going down as her hind feet. Leaving the ground had me breathless, I was so far up there. Flying and amazed and another language altogether.

Her hooves and the apocalypse, but not a horseman in sight. Darling, *ma chou,* it sounds right, *tu es dangereuse* I might have known. No wild horses but still dragged me away. For certain things I prefer her language, its continental sound. The impression of being there. Nonetheless I toss my head and think of the word "bridle," think it a seeming sound, the bit, but not so ever between my teeth.

Equestrienne, that feminine, I would that it were. Out of my chest, my heart it means nothing. They have a strange look. Horse and equestrienne, such a seeming sound, would that it were. Quickening split for that salty tongue, that other one, I still can't talk. I think about that, riding *française.* Always remember, but it's never the same.

And what's in a leg, besides a heel. A hock, a fetlock, a bone and hoof. A knee joint, bulging so delicate; the way they run astounding. Pounding my sleep. To see it again I touch my pillow, hearing their language, carefully worded, sure footed. For a hide such as, why not. Their speed and nowhere, sinking into that strangeness, but not of it, never it, never the same. No matter what desire. Yet could she trip up, brought down, I have only a mind for that.

That and this, where had been my was. At times, like unto a pack of hounds at sunset. Eating her dust, every bit. At times in boots and bowler hat, in imagination, as it were, in impatience, riding crop tapping against the leather. My mare, as it were, a leaping concept, and the reins out of my hands. Sinking into that strangeness, why not. At sunset, the sorrel insistent, might I say burnished, might I say braised with colour. Out of my hands her muscled neck, it is all—how you say—for the better.

Leap this now with my heels dug in. To the hills in thought, elsewhere. An idea. A fault. How desperate that colour with the light going and with mine own eyes. True to form. Thinking myself onto her back or hounding her dust it makes no headway. To the hills in thought where devils me still, in my sleep always riding or trying to talk. A simple concept, a quite promising fault. Wild horsing want, that sort of keen, but covered by another language, not to be understood. What to say if I am.

For the better; never the same. Horse and equestrienne. Equestrienne, my mare, how presumptuous; a leg up into the saddle and my empty hands. A simple concept, pounding my sleep. A stretch to cover, it meant not. I thought about brought down. Stop looking. An injured bone, hock, that fetlock tuft above the hoof.

I might have known. I might have said. My head tossed and some sound like her flying from my throat. Or this way perhaps, what do you think, my arms locked about her neck. The riding partaken, the style and instinct. Then what my weight upon her back.

LOFT

*(a mystery novel
in unmarked chapters)*

If that life hadn't been hers it never would have interested you. For what reason did you bed with her? Up there in the skylight she strung her hammock under panes of glass, where the light shone in all night. One searing floodlight, fixed to the roof, illuminating **SUPERIOR DRY CLEANING COMPANY** painted on the outside of the top of the elevator shaft. Something to see at night, something to face or turn away from, you spent some time thinking. How it came to be, and what reason there.

Last night through the heavy locked door. *No one knows I live here, no one is supposed to.* Up the ladder to the skylight. The city fanned out, dim, luminescent, and you drifting or suspended above it. On the roof. From here you could see the bridge and all it passed over, the dark and sleeping water. Smell of tar, still soft from the day's heat. Her hand joined yours just as she told you. The edges of the building. Over there, where the roof ended.

In the morning, a flood of other light. The hammock light of her and conforming your body. You wandered down into her space, saw her oil paints, her canvases, her clarinet's shine and gleam. This was different. She left evidence of herself all through her loft; there was always music and paint even when she wasn't there. There was the dust of her, her books, everything she had worn in the past month. There was no carpet anywhere, and the chair she had made with her own hands. There was something you couldn't touch, or take a name to, baffling and variform. It would drive you crazy to think. Beautiful and so baroquely lit, like rising from the head of a sleeping body. Her space. Her music. Her life on the roof.

*"No matter what I may have wanted,
I could tell she was not someone to graft onto myself."*
This from the beginning.

Facing or turning away from, you spend some time in contemplation. Where edge meets space. What you wanted of her. Repeated times through the heavy locked door, on the other side rising up and fanning out above the city. Like that painting you saw once: *Sleep*; the two sleepers melded, eyes closed, swirling in bedclothes and soaring through the dusky sky. With your hand in hers, rising from the head of a sleeping body. None knew you there. In that dark place, you made for yourself. Your hands had their interest of her, if she stood on the roof and approached that edge you wouldn't have to. How to stay safe, or turning away from. For this reason, you never talked purpose.

Enigmatic. Contiguous. The beauty of the words.

Her evidence testified for her: there was something, indeed, here. What you returned for, going far back as you could reach and she there or not. Something like that light, morning in through the skylight or the other window and filling the room below. Those were days you bedded upon it, strung up in the hammock, half-conscious, seeping, nurturing the inbetween. The chair she made with her own hands was something to hold you, you knew that at the time. At once. She'd had some knowledge of you, and where she got it. There were those words, like commencement, like origin. They came to head.

To head. Your head. Suspended where you could meet your match. That hammock on the light.

Thaumaturgy. She worked that magic and for all she had in her hands. In the ends of her dark hair. In this way she had it, that you were looking for and no matter what. You needed, and it was better if none knew you there.

It was hers and it interested you. She was doing. It could continue without you but she brought you in, she joined her hand to yours. She brought you in to her space and evidence, you could join with hers. It did interest you. If she could do what you wanted you wouldn't have to. For what reason did you draw close.

Those nights when it was hot, **SUPERIOR DRY CLEANING COMPANY.** You slept with her on the roof at times, and that light all night long. In all that city, none but you could see what it shone on, and by it, her skin and yours effulgent. None entered below, though you knew yourself both elevated and exposed. Sounds drifted through the elevator shaft; they were lost by the time they reached you, bearing no trace of their origins, you listened as long as you stayed conscious. Knowing her beside you, not knowing, her face in intent repose. Her spirit out there, under the bridge, floating on the face of the dark and sleeping waters.

*"It is possible
she may not be known to you
by the name on her birth certificate.
If threatened, she may have denied her knowledge."*

Where edge meets sleep. Knowing that her beside you. Knowing that she begrudged that one particular light, said she'd take a BB gun and shoot that light out, she'd give herself some darkness. What interested you: her brushes, her paints, her panes of glass, what you came to face with. She was always up before you and leaving her evidence. What you didn't have to. Every night you fought with this; in the depth of her hammock and what is hopeless. That she was not perhaps you or separate. That you could touch her in this, only in this, that most clumsy of ways.

There was the way she played her clarinet at night, it was something for her breath to pass through, it was something to hear. Each note high and clear and serially rising. Her fingers something to see to your eyes, each one knowing the keys.

It was beyond admiration. It was beyond question. Your talk of purpose, reason, all to yourself.

Crazy to think. One evening a bizarre turn of her head had you coming to grief. You knew it wasn't as they said in books. Untrue. Unspecified. This, here, was different; much more than the imperishable talk inside your head. She could put a stop to that, might fill it with her evidence instead. That you would contain this, the notion, her shards and particles, separate and partial and yet uncompleted. To head they came, baffling and variform just close to where your welcome was hot. Grasping. It seemed that you could: for a moment, in a while, at the time, or maybe later. You thought at bay with your techniques, thoughts of the depth of her hammock and the conformity of her arms, but there were those certain times and in peculiar ways. When it was dark—which there was never—she was very touching.

"It was then that I realized I could not trust whatever I said to her."

Out the heavy locked doors, down the hall, around the corner. The bathroom where she washed her hair in the sink at night, when the warehouse was empty. No one was to know. How to stay safe. The most habitual moves subject and consequential, none could tread here without a second thought. She entered in to the way you thought, she came with an assembly of distinction, confluence of definition and process; you were at her disadvantage and by the morning you both were lost. She left a mark, but not for all to see.

Her hair a dark and shining thing, cleansed in the sink, slicked to the shape of her skull. Still wet when she came back in through the doors. This, among others, a condition of her life on the roof.

Her music. Her art. Her panes of glass. She was so like that.

All admiration, trepidation, you come to face with a head full of craving. Time away from her space like nothing lived before. You are subtly altered. You are radically disturbed. You look the same to any around you. You go through your day, a still book of hours. You go through your day. To think that before she mattered, this did; to think that maddening. It was hers and that was why: your techniques and machinery. One evening the roof: you walked the perimeter. Soft tar on one side, the sheer drop to the city the other.

Purpose and reason, knowing that her beside you, is this the light. Compounded by her panes of glass. You watched her reflections at night; she was so many women, all separate all exactly the same. Purpose and reason, she let it lie. She turned in her hammock and the skylight glass, so many arms shifted and settled, so very much dark hair. Her face. Her traces. To have her do it for you, how dare you. She would neither confirm nor deny, she kept at least to herself. Herself and her so many reflections, is this, at last, the light.

Your head. Going as far back as you could reach, was she there. It had a start. Was she there and in what way, commencement and origin, the anvil of coming together. You wanted this time. Did you. You thought it could happen, you had those thoughts both elevated and exposed. Did you. Talking purpose to forfeit your safety, that was what you never accomplished. You took her evidence as your own, you left her mark and she let you. And how, no matter what, if nothing else, for all intents and purposes, you are confused.

Fighting the depths. Here you discover an ultimate vertigo, that nothing is so straight up and down. For all the knowledge you had of her you were perpetually unprepared. For all her evidence. She brought you in, but what had she done, how had she ensured your complicity. To everything she was herself. She was. You drank in the influence of her subtle directives.

There was never any way that would stay safe. In your dream you meet your match, the edges of that warehouse building. In that most clumsy of ways. Once the sun was up the only tangible thing you had of her was her evidence, was she there. Soaring through the dusky sky or falling, something to face or turn away from.

"You understand, of course, I mean myself."
None other.
But which of us is she.

How gentle, you are confused.

The conditions of her life on the roof. It was something to pass through, your breath, your fingers. The self-conscious vertigo, drifting through the elevator shaft. Absorbed in her traces. None knew you there, no one was supposed to: you rose up without witness, up there above the city. Almost. Seeping. She was something to miss, she did it nearly; she was so like that. What you did by her, in this, as everything: the beauty of the words. If anything.

MISSION:
a nineteenth-century romance

Nothing more treacherous than a biographer with a mission. Back then is a way of thinking. Without a doubt. In this comparative literature, the word "consumption" is more romantic than "tuberculosis," one implying fire and danger, the other, bacteria. A relationship of excess to mind. The entrance of subjects gives us something to worry about. Call them Frederic Chopin, George Sand. If I'm more infected by people of the previous century than by others, it's because they are so much more easily manipulated. Thirty-eight years of age and depressed to heartbreak over the rupture, I refocus mourning to a blue, sharp here and then. When dead people split up, it seems to be forever. Manipulation. I can't let go of it. George Sand and Chopin took action, but I could undo it. I can reconcile each to the other, my hand up to the wrist in the dark manifold of what we call what really happened and fucking it up.

Fucking history. The perversion lies in the craftsmanship. My research is more penetrating than your research, and I'm really worried now. Because I have to, I peep in biographies for a version to live with. Some say Chopin was homosexual except when he was sleeping with George. The refocussing of orientation is needed for any grasp at all. George knew what she was getting into, and got right into it. I said so. "I have spent my heart in the strangest arms"—which one of us said that? Talking, and we have so many thoughts. In the nineteenth century, we spoke a language between piano and pen, but now we are ill and our words are put to hard uses. Excess to mind. Looking at himself in the curvature of George's dark eyes, Chopin pondered whose reflection he was seeing and knew it was himself through her projector. One fuck of a funhouse mirror.

Lifestory is a metaphor for these other stories. Reconciliation is a way of thinking. There's licence. A middle ground inhabited by biographers, pathological liars, bagmen. Who says I wasn't there. This is where we come into our own: our chance to make an impression. If I can stretch back across 148 years to the place where his breathing is hardest, I'll do it. Who's to say I wasn't present at Chopin's death, when everyone in Paris claims he died in their arms? I have arms too, and they can be found in the strangest places. Once he'd breathed his last, I took the diligence and rode 180 miles to George at Nohant, and if she didn't exactly throw herself into my arms we at least spent the night in a kind of comfort. Thoughts of lips, and sentimental rubato, but someone here is lying.

Bereft on his deathbed, Chopin: "She told me I would die only in her arms." Impetus for staying out of them, but he never stopped grieving for it. One evening in the middle of an asthma attack, George put her arms around me and murmured in my ear, "Darling, I can feel your chest bubbling." It didn't stop her from carrying matters to a point later that night, or nothing stops me. In any version of history, again and again, I throw myself on the mercy of the unhealthy. Consumption or bacteria, it's all the same in the grave. We know which makes better copy.

Which one of us said *that?*

If I say he did die in her arms, and you haven't been reading around, you aren't to know the difference. What stands between them now but a pack of biographers. There's space enough for company. So much can be arranged. I have suffered infection before, and it always comes to this. Burning out to a contentious juncture. There are endings out of existence and I have so many. Comparative literature. Multiple choice.

RENÉE VIVIEN

(or, a fable of fashion)

1899. Given the clothes they wore, just how did they begin to make love, each to each? First, hands rising to remove the decorative cartwheel hats from their hair, which massed about the crowns of their heads. Their hands reaching behind their backs, a posture for slender arms, hands unhooking hook from eye, hook from eye, till gown begins to loosen and slide. Bared shoulders. Gracing petticoats. The delicate problem of negotiation: whalebone stays. Hooks and eyes reprised, or laces? The dexterity of hands—each to each. Love, indeed, intriguing at the time.

One is bent the century demands; how to fix in this one? Through recitation, on paper, by plagued and influenced memory. How gracefully she becomes that thought. How horribly she passed. What sort of sigh was sounded as the stays were loosened? We may not know, we may perhaps never. How disturbing: her books cannot be found.

Cause of death: a surfeit of gin and unrequited love.

Infinitely graceful, imminent. Wary at the century's turn. But falling (in any case) for an arm around the shoulder, a pair of lips and bouquets of flowers (tied by the stem, the way of all flesh) forgetting and forgetting. She for whom the word "swoon" was created, who said *"the infinite charm of desire and regret."* A swoon is but a little death. Death was fashionable. We were meant to be attractive. As beauty was meant to be broken.

Cause of death: lack of a name for what the matter was. Those gowns. Their heaviness. Weighted down with gorgeous embroidery, crimped sleeves. Her waist most grievously dealt with. And one might see bared shoulders, but naught but the tips of her shoes, and she as her as she could be. She was, herself, all flesh.

There are her books, succulent with femininity and decay. The surviving fragments. One never has the whole. We have perfume, and an air of her gallantry. Flowers, suggestions of fragrant flesh. The desire for the nunnery. She put it on paper. Or, as they say, one woman to another. Making of her a thousand refractions that may perhaps never. And translated to high-buttoned boot.

And given the times, just how did she publish? Her verses so untempered, wicked and delicious. *La belle epoch.*

Allowances were made and it helped to be wealthy. She was, and yet. Decadence was all the rage, but she was serious. Therefore, deserving: living long enough to see her books disused. She did, and yet; how early she passed.

At the turn of a century, the turn of a mind, though the body still held by whalebone stays. A new century should have been something. Freedom should have meant survival; pleasure.

    Young women of the future. Pleasure: an undulating word, the mind turning, the body curving. Young women. Slipping out of the past—out of time, and place. Dreaming at night and dressing each morning. There was going to be movement, desire, and pleasure. Pleasure and desire: the coming hundred years.

    Swooning they come, along that path. Those young women—think of it. Each one worth the paper she was written on. She loved one for the brazen colour of her hair, called another divinely blonde, adored the romance of yet another's pale slim hands. No beauty could be left unsung: for her, the nunnery would have to wait. Chastity had the allure of peace, but she was serious. Desiring desire to be pure—could not one dress in white instead? And what could not be made of passion, the hottest fires to purify best.

Cause of death: lack of an ecstatic speculative blueprint.

Given the times, just how did she avoid marriage? It too was a fashion, and had its imperatives. It helped to be wealthy and have accommodating chaperones. Charming one's parents was an alternative. To go so far, and know certain gestures, or have instead the sudden demise of one's father—a questing, parentless freedom. It helped to trust to the future, the swooning, the young women of the future society.

The delicate problem of negotiation. Each marriage avoided was a step toward pleasure, a chance to lift another's heavy armful of satin. And touch her gorgeous embroidery. But how, then, was it to be? Hook and eye, hook and eye, till gown begins to loosen and slide? To high-buttoned boot. Till death do you part.

Cause of death: exposure to Baudelaire at too early an age.

The density of a lifted armload of satin, in a century that loved remorse. Such preoccupations. Forward movement is imperative—a sip of gin steadies the hand. In doffing an entire century, she would need a muster of nerve. Or be weakened to the point of abandonment—stunned: seeing and believing it, but not living. Yet, may not a young woman in love with death take a detour? In turn-of-the-century photographs, skin is always perfect and luminous. Something is preserved. Perhaps regret was what was desired. Falling. She was always falling. She might say *"Being love's slave, what could I do but wait upon the flowers and tides of its desire?"* How to fix in this one.

Recitation, paper, plagued and influenced memory. Such unseemly verse. Those insistent works. To love that way was all the rage, but only if one didn't mean it. That way, indeed, could engender many things. Swooning young women; desire and pleasure; that undulation. Meant to be broken. She was all flesh, and well worth the paper she was written on.

Succulent femininity, and decay. An armload of satin, and a foot in the grave. There are those who find that attractive. Many. But how to love them? This was never laid out. Something for poetry to plot—disturbing that her books cannot be found. The surviving fragments: a young Englishwoman writing in French. The French translated back into English. What could she have meant? Love, indeed, intriguing at the time.

But how to love them? *"They tortured me so unintentionally and so gracefully!"* What could she have meant? Their hooks, their eyes, how early she passed. Within a decade of the coming hundred years, starved for lack of a name for what the matter was. She did, and yet. The young women about her, in her arms, on her paper. For whom was the century meant? That one following the one in love with remorse.

Definition might lie within those fragments, sifted through two languages, a fountain pen, and gin. And nonetheless, they might be words. How to love them, to fix in this one. Those from her hand, that mind at the turn of the century. In the next life, no matter what she said, she would purify best. Desire and regret go on forever, it is a kind of preservation, indifferent to the numbered years. Bouquets of flowers, tied by the stem, the way of all verse. Suffering a concept in battered history.

Cause of death: a pathological fondness for the nocturnes of Chopin.

Dressing in white is no excuse, though indeed it is lovely. The hottest fires may purify best. There were always arms enough. There was always remorse enough. Engaged with this, enough rough music, the rustle of a petticoat descending or swept overhead. And how, shall we ask, in that time, were we enjoined to be fashionable, to love remorse? To say it was in the air, it was assumed, it was desirable, is not without truth. Is not unlike a tale. Bred to whalebone stays. She was most grievously dealt with.

A plunge into the next century. A deep breath, and a prodigious feat. Which was not done. The coming hundred years, which loved not remorse.

To fix in this one. To may perhaps never. Staying power—a concept in battered history. How to begin to make love. There were her books to may perhaps never; they told of a distant turn, and the divinable future, spinning through a double language. To speak of deathly fashion. What was meant, and how to love them *so grace-*

fully and unintentionally! Insistent works. Fragments. Desirous of a speculative blueprint.

What sort of sigh was sounded as the stays were loosened? Such preoccupations. If another could choose her own last words, they might be *"The tobacco flowers were soothing the violet dusk with their perfume of sleep. Their breath of insidious langour inspired ambiguous dreams."* Meaning precisely. Slipping time, and come along that path. Ways and times for a particular being.

FOUR POSTCARDS ON A THEME

PIZZA AT HER PLACE

How she kills them. Nostalgia. By candlelight, roaches. No wall too vertical, white plaster, black baseboard paint in the down of downtown. Where she lived before the crash, apocalypse among the debris. Pestilence, and her apartment put to the fist and boot.

    Maître d'-style crossing the street. Recall. Before 2 A.M., you want it, they deliver. Pizza joint opposite her apartment building but she gets them to come to her: assistant chef makes good by cutting across the middle of the dark street, white apron, pizza box balanced in one hand. Politics of the Hawaiian Special through the facts of Third World pineapple production. She can tell you where each ingredient came from. Eating guilt and more, she hates herself with every bite and still her teeth maul the crust. You don't stop. Tomato sauce, ham, pie dough. Hours, just to see her teeth break the smooth cheese surface. Taken with her beauty and madways over the top as romance makes its ingress. One heartfelt fuck-up after another.

Not the wine, not the talk, but the pizza vanquished from its box, scuttle crumbs, residual foodsmell on the air. Bare-handed. One-handed. From the corner of her eye, locked on the crawling, palm cupped, wall thumped and roach dropping from air-pressure shock. Killed but untouched, primed for the morning sweep-up. She sprays a ring around the mattress on the floor. Raid. Inhabiting the inner circle, you, she, and what you wouldn't brave for her. Vermin, and the primitive. Troubled. Wherever her arms are, and close to her more.

Time passing and desperate, via exponential growth in the insect world. Can she prevail. Obstinate and siege. If she didn't sleep or used two hands; passing, the epoch of tranquil pizza. Furied, how now she eats her troubled and more. They come and come, crunch-shelled, indifferent, impassable than ever between you and her. Fist through the wall, fist through the glass to nothing swept up in the morning. Squeezing out, she throws her apartment in a box and gone. Her arms. Her more.

Wander, wander, bitch and rancour. Couple of years, the old street gone trendy whiling her absence. Stays the same the pavement, pizza joint across the way. Perpetual, vague and disturbing, empty pizza-box scent.

NO-ONE'S-LAND

If she says so. Remember. Her hair against blue denim. It's late in autumn, she's talking. What's coming down now, baby, and it ain't leaves. She's travelling somewhere via mind, and you weren't asked to come along. She says it's for the best, she knows you know she knows you, better than you know yourself. So listen.

Listening. And then there's listening. Where you stop the mind and become all ears. Tonight there'll be a harvest moon, and then you'll separate the wheat from the crap. You wonder, autumn means what in Kenya, India, Malaysia? You know where you are, and what it's like here.

Knew you were in trouble. You arrived in the broad P.M. and you could see that she was far off. In the no-one's-land of come here, go away. She does the damnedest. Takes advantage of a shaft of noonlight to hope you'll understand by putting her head in your lap. You're stuck with this. You know that from now on, whenever someone leaves, you'll remember her putting her head in your lap, hair wandering across your thighs, each strand coated with sun. She's done it again, and knows you can't get angry. You think, If only I could put some space between.

Tough-at-heart. Shoved your dignity in your pocket with the cigarettes and walked quiet out the door. Five minutes finds yourself standing in the transit station, crying by the map of the subway. It's better, underground.

You know you're going home, but just now your vocabulary lacks a word for it.

Map of the globe, rounded up and flattened out, divided like pie. Anywhere you cut it, it's still November. Hell of a country, that.

RITUAL

Every summer she cuts her hair short, leaving you defenseless, silent against the bones of her face and shoulders. Tank-top, and her arms beyond sculpture. Loves black. Never acquires a tan. Soft clothes on skin, each year you could believe it but she'll never know.

Heat, speed, lust. Bucket-seat leather searing the backs of your thighs. Pausing each red light to glean the fall of her shin, the narrow foot on the passenger side floor. Mistake to the beach, her tank-top, her shorts less than ever. You think, damned be all marriages. Anything like them. Playing holiday from her lover, and intimacies you don't want to know about. What frustrates your fingers to her cheekbone, jawbone, collarbone. Touch sand instead. SPF 30 but still, you're burned.

Slipshod style, elegance in water or on land. A disquiet ocean surface and her eyes are that blue. They do it to you. She talks, and you could embrace her persuasion: the unmitigated clarity of her face where she's down in the sand, lying on your blanket. Every year, and nothing changes. Even if you kissed her now, you know who she'd still go slouching toward by nightfall. When things cool off and heads prevail.

Marvelling the fit of her feet in her sandals. Her ignorance, you not revealing. You learned that somewhere. Getting a grip. Nothing but swimsuits between and she knows nothing. Change of weather and you might feel okay again. Her hair longer. Herself covered.

STILL TRAVELLING

80 KPH. A kiss is just a kiss. You're all friends, in an '81 Chevy. Driving south through black ink. You're one of three faces in a rent-a-wreck car, no stars, no moon but enough light for you to reckon out your place. In the back seat, behind their joined hands.

Three days at their house. Sunlight, butter on scones fresh out of the oven. On the waterfront, wave after wave hitting the sand. A fire in the wood stove every evening to warm the talk. Serene. Where you could believe in lovers and friends if only you weren't the one sleeping solo each night.

Alchemy of the unrequited. Long ago, one night in another country, you sat with her in the back of a taxicab, holding her hand. Watching the passing street lamps strobe her face. Electrified and fading, over and over, engine sound, sound of heart. If you could have any out-of-body experience, you'd pick this one: to be sitting in the driver's seat in the here and now, in charge of the wheel, and her at your elbow. Step on the gas. Nudge the pedal a few kilometres faster to drop off the passenger in the back and be alone with her again. Hell bent for nowhere.

At the ferry docks, outside the car, you and her companion embrace and peck cheeks; but still. In her arms you shy from her lips. What means so little. You know she doesn't notice.

Spent, by the time the ferry landfalls on the far side of the passage. Sleep-wanting, still travelling. Middle of night.

MUSIC, SWEET & COLD

*That was not natural. A way of hearing,
and of expressing. That mode of hearing
involved the whole self—*

One's own strangeness concerns one's self. From childhood one played, and grew in the shadow of that gift. Before one's hand could cover an octave. A condition of difference, isolation claims its own. Disastrous, and wholly desirable. So much came far in advance—unsettlingly so. One needed to hold back. As it is, those fingers now are gone for good. The speaking parts were superimposed on one another; different, settling about each other, and not meeting. There were always numerous questions. *Do you want to find out?* A perplexing shyness afflicts one's footsteps: wherever one goes, one can never relent. On stage and in private, one knew one's self strange. Hearing, in fact, was an end in itself; and one heard in that way—and couldn't explain it.

Perhaps if one could keep to one's self, something could stay protected. Why tell it at all.

The hands, though, were prodigious communicators: those who heard them, loved them dearly. An audience of watchers called them fragile; the hands were personal, rarely seen, and shocking. Untouched, and under command, one's hands, at least, are particularly one's own. One need not extend them. Occasionally, in perversity, sometimes the hands reach out against one's will. Sometimes it hurts: it's worse than one could think. They loved them dearly, those who bruised them. Some were in this much gratified.

The music again was another method. It summoned attention, emerging from under the fingers so lucidly, though it was not what any thought. It was cryptic. It could seem exotic. Gently insistent: think again. Listen. Why be the portrait any would expect?

One had an unusual face. One had a tenuous body. One was, in one's way, all hands. All hearing.

Hearing in truth was an end in itself. The most bizarre species of confusion. Gradually one became aware of one's breath, and shuddering body, and knew the phrase "to thrill." There at the keyboard. That peculiar way of touching with the wrists lowered, the fingers flat. One knew one's self strange; it occurred in no other manner. This was to have been kept a private thing: alienation, in the extreme of one's gift.

Public or private, sweet and cold. *Saying those things. Sound game.* Stage persona—perhaps a tactic. A pure way to defend one's self: bafflement. *Exposed. Every time, stepping on stage. Groaning through the motions.* What is one doing? One must ask the question, for one finds one's self strangely. A stage like that was a matter of course, one took it as it came, but the performance stayed surely a dark one. It was shyness, perhaps. It was dread. One's defences were needed: one marshalled illusion. If one can stand outside one's self, one need not stand aware.

Sweet and cold, one plays one's personality, each track over and under its self. The sound of this was deliberate polyphony. Those seeming parts were what they heard, those who were baffled; those who thought they knew. *Much of an age. Do you want to find out?* It was a conflict, yes, the strain was there. One feared it desperately. One had such a way with one's hands, but no way to think of it; one feared to think of it.

In time, this would become "a detrimental element."

One became in private what one knew. One could feel one's hands moving in the slow parts carefully. That was subtle, and touching. The flesh vibrated. One's listening was thrilling: oh, so: how the sound responded.

One needed to hold back. There were uneasy rituals to be performed; the concert life: from performance to performance and other venue. The world, and a stage. An undivined tactic.

Standing outside had been such a desire. Never so greatly divided. One's "likeness to" was a likely surface; one had an act to play. One kept one's ecstasy under cover. *Live ones, out there. The inescapable numbers. Hostility.* One's gift: pinioned, examined. One wanted escape, one plotted and played, one sought for barriers. These were days of gruelling to please; one's spirit broke in so many forms, and troublingly often.

A condition of difference: isolation. Now thousands would watch but who could notice? *All, or none.* That charming surface had contradictions. Its difference left little other choice. This had become all too necessary.

In secret and in death, wedded to that sound . . .

If one could stand outside one's self, one need not extend one's self. There were others, always there, always wanting in. Sooner or later, one was expected to make contact, sustaining nothing less than one's anomalous bruised hands. *And into what could this lead?* A form of protection was one's surface, a kind of charm. Certain. Within the variants of sweet and cold, sweet and cold, one sensed one's self at odds. Oddly one played, and others listened. It was a form, a model; one would keep it all one's days, even after one had left the stage. For good. For all. It was a time to keep one's distance; one could only stand so much.

Within the extreme of one's own gift, the scale and

measure. Immersion in it caused its exigency. What did one have on one's hands? Indeed, at such times, one looks to it strangely, one is much of an age after all. So many watchers had their comments. *To hell.* One could say, "This is not unusual." One would be lying. Occasionally, now, one considered one's hands, how far they had brought. So much in advance. *As far as all that?* And how. It was almost a mistake, it was like a mistake. One's gift was what one could not compass. How was one to grow, other than strange—one's protective layers, applied or grown, one by one.

Difference, among other things. A way of hearing, a way of expressing. Through the hands. That was not natural. Nor suppressible. So many strands could emerge, sounding individually, and simultaneously. Not all heard by anyone else; that division was sharp. It never left. That mode of hearing involved the whole self: one rocked, one swayed, one sweated. Disastrous it was, and wholly desirable.

One's uncommon hands were a site of anxiety. Reticent, and difficult. There were those things one couldn't touch. Not that one wished, but at certain times how could one stay one's wonder? A pure way to defend one's bafflement, and sometimes sensing that other phrase. *Do you want to find out?* Need one trade one for the other? State of perplexity. Chemistry. One had a body. One sensed the mockery: *Darling, how charming one's touch-shy ways.*

A stage like that was a matter of course; one took it as it came. The performance a dark one. But one's hands were diffident, wanting one way and moving another. Baffling and lying, one sensed one's self at odds. Tremendously gifted, and touchingly estranged.

Detrimental elements that sound together; from time to time in fetching complexity. One thought as if one might. One was much of an age. Yet one's diffident hands and tenuous body, slip-jointed, slouch-shouldered, strange and afflicting: extreme. An end in itself. One can never relent.

Let alone. To experience one's strangeness one had only to start talking; the consolling and bruising, burgeoning distance. Those who listened, heard otherwise. One's words never quite reached, but the distance was inhabited, coldly, bleakly, and with frustrating elegance. One knew this intimately, and it was somewhat gently wounding. One made that choice long ago. Saying those things.

Such was that distance. This too was fragile. Beyond that distance, the sound of their voices. Compelling. Disturbing. From the lip of the stage, an aqueous murmuring. Coldly and bleakly one set about one's unease, finding one's hands through the slow parts, one's body. It was not to have been for public unravellment—yet one needed what soothing one had to offer.

The frustrating elegance of one's own hands. Their confounding sensitivity. So could they not be lenient. One thought, and trembled. One had already lost through them what one could only imagine. *Mind this is, once a tenuous body.* Not for touching, these, *but the bruising might be sweet* the very thought of losing out. One was born and bent a certain way. One used one's hands as one must.

Mockery, only, to make a life complete. How necessary. How touching. Past a certain point, the choice was made. Shy unto death. Those never-reaching words. But sweet the bruising, how sweet, how sweet—

One kept it all one's life, always sensing that other phrase. Comes a time when it could not have been otherwise. The way one heard. The way one was bent. From beyond the edge, the voices. Under one's hands, the keyboard. One's difference left little other choice.

One left the stage. One protected one's hands. Strange in one's ways, all music, all hearing.

*And to be sure that was a foot she held in her hand:
bruised and raw, confounded by its treatment*

SHOES

She said, "You must be a dancer, for you have long hair, and arch supports within your shoes." I had a fancy, just then. Rubber on cement. Bastard, upstart, boulevard walk. Taking the steps, big wide stride, and she said, "perfect size 7." Her face; I was overheels in love, all the way up to the ankle.

Right or left foot, on or off. It's one thing and another, just whatever you want. Cabaret shoes or spikes, a.k.a. come-fuck-me heels, but I prefer lace-up ankle boots just like the kind grandma used to wear. The smell of leather: must be. It put me onto this. Could be. Perfect step, wicked stride: I'd put up with the calluses, no question, worth it, damn right, fuck-you-too, laces running through half a dozen eyelets and crossing over and over a high, hard instep. Mine. Maybe my feet looked like that to her. God only knows what she saw.

But it was long hair and arch supports, at first glance. It does make for illusion. Romance. Kid leather is much, much softer. She was holding my foot, and that was an advantage. Yes, I would say. I am hard on my shoes. How quickly the heels grind down, turfed-onto-the-sidewalk shufflin' dance. I've been doing it for so long I don't know any better. Dancing shoes really break the skin. Cowboy boots would suit me fine.

Heel first, then toe, then do it again. I can move like that. Love the old expression, "the balls of your feet." If you need to turn that's where to do it. The quicker you move, the less you blister. Under the arch, a little neoprene, and feels like you could walk all day, fancy that if you need to. Nothing like an attitude to set you making tracks.

Footgear's the way to go. Leather over foundling bones. Early mornings, slipping into my escape shoes, the ones I keep by the door. These come in women's sizes, with a suppleness of sole. No need for socks. I've gone places with them, can't stay light-foot enough. One up, one down. The way of the world, all toughshit and roughstuff, enough to impress, anyway, but it's looks that count, believe you me. From here on in. In the dark, ask me, the smell of leather and wax become sweeter than believable. Those fingers wrapped round my foot my "perfect size 7" could be almost anyone's. Up to the ankle, they were easy to take. Bastard, upstart, boulevard walk. A real shame, you bet, between rubber and cement.

Brazilian leather, or maybe Italian. One costs a lot more, a whole hell, but just try to get out without paying. Back in the stockroom, boxes and boxes of shoes to the ceiling make wicked soundproofing. It's private; things happen. There's a door that leads to the back. Deadpan alley; just my luck. Getting out there was a shock, cowboy boots, straight-faced and all, but the fit might not be perfect. The look is to die for: embossed bootleather all the way to the knee. Glue and stitching hold it to the sole.

SUB-ROSA

Gentle merger. Face—warm? Closer. Palm over sweat *ah good* kind of thought. Body temperature. Sub-
conscious. Web of lights goes out to difficult places. Someone on mine? Timing. Kiss. Purpose. Deal. Here, why not, for what. No kidding.

Dearly beloved, and insanely overted. And you that someone, is it not? I presume? No more than the closure of aperture, and then a door? Coming through, they say, walkabouts. For what, again. See: This: *I was here.* Greed glues on, it glitters and clews. Back to that palm, like palm over touch, being, as it were, sub-
aerial, and liking it too. Face—rosaceous. Saying this takes more than doing. And then a door. More fool you to la-dee-dah open.

Face? Face?? Face. *ah thank god* and who else, them who was here. Don't tell that part again. Kind of thought gentle anger, back to kiss again *oh good* and whose lips these are I think I know. But I presume. Roseate colour, of shame, of blaze, of dying-down-type fire and don't take them away, not now, for their own good. Pay me off, and in kind, and in lightning-tough sites. "Of all the rocks and the hard places in the world, ya had to land between mine."

Sub-

stance for a while, posture and joust. At faceside is an ear and whisper sashays up to it. Seeking to more the palm over sweat and stay with that heat, but susurrance sweeps me away. Carries me off. Loses my head. Waltzes me dingo. With greed glued on I prance those steps and room for more when I'm finished, but this is a stance of mine too, and I think you have word of it.

Body temperature. There, too. Warming the whisper, heat is a message. Well, but. And then a door, to sensual rosulation, sub-

ordinate rocks and hard, hard places, get along like oh, eh, um. More fool you, but you did, didn't you? Face aflame, heart booting; is this any way to run a railroad? Sort of. Kind of thought gentle merger, kind of thought kind of kiss, kind of merger gentle kiss. Gentle kiss. Back there *ah thank god* in terms of warmth you can't steam faster. Which, says I, rises from the body all the time. Thus was our steam placed together, side by each, one atop the other, that condensation might be mulched and blendered.

Have a hard time holding on to it, sub-

sidence to dew, or sweat, which do you prefer? One waltzing dingo for the road. Insouciant stepping. Tail chase; chaos we strive for. Rises from the body, says I, all-over-the-mapping and a time you'll have of it, too. Whisper susurrates the spiralling ear. I'd do anything, say anything, you have word of it. Dingoing steadily, and liking it too.

Hard time holding on to it. It is so damn beautiful in difficult places. Web of lights, and purposes. Not red, really, but rufescent. I was there, eh? *ah. oh.* It seems I was more than just warm, and I suppose you were watching. Sashayed up to it with glittering greed, sub-

orned by arrested intentions, or maybe not, maybe something gentler, and kissier. Threads of difficult light. It was not all bad, you know. Not at all. The way we run our little railroad.

I must, it seems, construe *thank god* and willy-nilly. What the dingo for the road, who the lips, and posture, and joust. Under whose steam, and overmapping. To where the railroad. The difficult places, and palm over sweat. The sheer rose-istance of it all, sub-

ject to its own laws and customs. Web of lights, winking and fooling, ah yes, me too.

Attend me now, ye insanely overted. No kidding. I want what I had, and strive to stay with it. Remembrance, the things present, all taxes in. The kiss may come too hard, but I'll give it a place to land; a shame not to feed dying-

    down-type fire. My face was blazing, as any could see.

Sashay kissier ah me too, it's almost a place to live. 'Way

      downunder, we call everyone "mate" with impunity. That's just the way we do it, while topside we pass for normal. Jiggered and damned. Liking it too.

Taste that dust from the last tail chase. Never said it would be, well, you know. And fools construed. Never said but presumed. Body temperature keeps things lively, what? Sub-

      junctive as all get-out. And pretty personal too, but you always managed to sink in.

More than just warm. As were my rocks, hard places. Paid off. Blendered. And that too I like. Dingo to go.

WHISKEY SOUR

Thousands of people and those two. Hell of a night. It rains suddenly here, at the centre of late afternoon and a great warm downpour. The streets humid at night, a good place to find you, but not the last place you slept. Save it for later. Clothes sticking to your skin. On the sidewalk you hear everything, why not sax or muted horn or all those voices. All at once. The two of them, dark and blond and lovely drawls but they did not say they were from here. The two of them, all at once. Dark and crazy. Music from the jazz joints all along the street, falling into it, one screaming riff after another, what difference is there. Some vacation. The steaming city on the Gulf.

That there would be two, who could tell? Close up, they are continuously beautiful. Those faces. Anything to keep looking, already calling the darker one *mon joli:* this that kind of city, French and American, a city that heartens licence. Perhaps you were afraid.

When the touching started. Sitting in the outdoor café just barely out of the sun, both of them sharing your side of the table. One, and then the other. From shoulder to hand, to hip and thigh, neither hiding what he was about from the other. The heat keeps you calm despite your peaking excitement, drifting off, spiking once more, rush after rush, thinking they couldn't possibly see, this too intense and particular. *You didn't. You can't.* How vivid your hands, one hand working a coffee cup or spoon, the other always touching someone else. The sounds of dishes, people from inside the café. It went on a long time at the aluminum table behind the wrought-iron railing before the blond leaned over and kissed you, then drew back softly while the dark one took his place even before you opened your eyes again. Their kisses distinct as fingerprints.

Despite peaking excitement, your body at rest. Your mind endlessly rising from that chair, going a long way up. Change is inescapable. Closed eyes, feeling the heat, the hands. And the kisses now, each starting before the end of the last, one and the other. This happening, but no decision made. This is, must be, what is called acquiescence.

Un croissant for breakfast. *Il fait très chaud,* you think. A sky growing heavier and lower as the day goes on. *Occur. Did. Yes. Actually. It did. It did.*

Jack Daniel's with a twist of lime. On the rocks, in the glasses from the bathroom of your hotel room. You and the two of them, sitting on the bed playing a lazy, well-known entertainment, one cube going from lips to these lips, melted ice slipping from other to other. Still and forever, their hands a warm multitude. When at last the clothes come off, yours go first. Their smooth hard bodies to the waist and then rough fabric against your skin. When he rises to slip from his jeans the other comes into your arms and deeper inside. How vivid your hands at the back of his neck. And the first one, the darker one, looks on in silence.

This, then, was not imagined. The door to the balcony left open and the rain roaring down into the city. Your thighs ache, your lips, their hair damp with sweat. Dark, blond. How such arms and legs can intertwine, no end to it. Those were your hands, but in a different place. And now with those two. You left the bed for the chair, where still they sought you out, that one with his arms around your hips, his mouth on your thighs. Still more. Going to shower and being caught by the first at the bathroom door and no time to you riding him, his back to the floor tiles and water streaming from your hair and body. The certainty that every outcry would be the last. And still once more.

The decision made, everything tilting. Your sleep was long to bring you into night; their promise to come together after midnight at the jazz joint. To bring yourself to faith. Already now, it hadn't happened. But after the second shower, after room service for one, after dressing, what else could you do.

Steaming city on the Gulf. The street pastiche all the way to the club and all those voices, your clothes sticking to your skin. All the way, on faith. Until you enter the club and see them through blue smoke and sound of brass, seated at a table with an open bottle and a third glass between them. You slip into place. Kiss like lovers; this chaotic, eccentric music.

This too intense and particular. Maybe you were afraid. As much the city as anything else; composed of decaying cathedrals, jazz. Simmering weather; dark business. So courted and plundered, just waiting for it makes it possible. And that striking number, each an angle to have it given back. Lust's provender; miraculous patience. One takes over where the other stops, *a dark nervy business* startling dilation *happened* an adjustment demanded *actually happened* intoxicating, insistent and bitter. *Afraid for the first time* finding yourself in that city *was afraid* predicting you would always come to this. Making you something else to go back to.

The two of them, dark and blond and lovely drawls—what their matter? Their common ground. Between agitated breaths (damp hair falling across their eyes) they say, *"It's the only way, and it almost never happens."*

Conceivably, the heat makes all seem acquiescence. Chaotic music, narcoticized equilibrium. And given the climate, skin so accessible. Sweat runs all together. May you not be forgiven, might you, for slipping out of yourself? *Given the circumstances. In view of events.* The better you not spare that matter.

On account of the rain, the air is heavy at night, the pavement shining. Even now, at 4 A.M., this city sweats, where the boys are, their effeminate beauty, the second floor of the low-rise. Where they are living, or staying. Boys like that, young men, who have kept something of secrecy, where they grew from. Barely remembered, wedded strength and grace.

What a number you make. What a picture. Leaving their bed, you grab *mon joli's* T-shirt and toss it over your head, hitting you mid-thigh. Dressed *comme les boys,* stepping out onto their balcony, the wrought iron looking frail as lace, hard as nails. From here they could be lovers, slung together on the bed and slacked out in sleep. From here they could be brothers in beauty and expression. This astonishing dilation. What have you. The exhilaration and moments of insupportable pleasure *it's the only way* it isn't right *it so seldom happens* you are not from here.

Saved for later. A breath of heavy night air. A glimpse of dark foliage, and dim lights. He draws you back into the room and, still standing, pushes his T-shirt to your waist. Your legs lock round his hips, your arms around his shoulders to lever your body. From the bed the other watches. Waits.

There is *grande café* at the Café du Monde. Coffee, whipped cream, chocolate, powdered sugar—such ruinous plenty. It is recommended (to tourists) that one put on a raincoat to consume it; the very thought of a raincoat—in your present situation—making you shudder with silent laughter. *After this, how to be.*

The last time you slept. Maybe days ago at your hotel, in the afternoon, the sound of the air conditioner keeping everything out. *Didn't.* Do Not Disturb on the door. *Can't.* The clarity of their skin brought a certain ease of mind, one florid, one olive. If they weren't so new. So unseasoned. If you were tough and cynical. The passage of your sleep from blond hair to dark and darker eyes. Dreaming that when you sleep with them, you fall easily to each other, all touching some part of that other.

Enough to go round. How much of you, after all, is there. Some tiny edge inside, and now you know. *This is, must be.* Perhaps it cannot be got over. Sleep tipping to nightmare, struggling now as you turn in your sleep. Begin again. The third part of the number, you make it possible. What, after all, is acquiescence. Predicting you would come to this.

The sleep that happened so many miles from here—what that composition? *How does one; how can one?* How vivid your hands. Why not sax or muted horn or those two. These were always conceivable.

City of mind and body, to keep and compass. To be compressed within the brain, where it really cooks. Where it really works. *As my darlings go, these are better than most.* Say something cool and self-possessed. *Than any.* As a vantage point, this is not bad. Perhaps in fact, the most complete.

Then what now for didn't and can't. One takes over where the other stops. Fear, synthesis and astonishing dilation. *When it's hot like this* you think *wear only cotton.* Now then for happening, a dissolving, unclimbed edge. For Jack Daniel's with a twist of lime.

Boys like these to remind you of others, brothers, lovers. Desire was to come and go, its cessation bringing something like repose. But nothing comes to rest. Desire for one thing segues to something other (predicting you would always) how much of you is there. Shape-shifting and constant, restless as hell.

Some vacation. To bring yourself to faith, this steaming city on the Gulf, and the multitude of their hands. Coming for the music and finding their hands on your legs, across your belly and shoulders and touching your face. Happening; it hadn't happened and yet once more. The endless repetition of desire. Their serene faces on either side of you, their dark and blond in evening light, keeping you calm.

As much the city as anything else, dark and crazy, waiting makes it possible. Your hands at the back of one's neck. Your legs around one's hips. Maybe you were afraid; constant and nervy and thinking. How much there is.

It almost never happens. And if it did? The insupportable: to get on. During the last day, you never leave the hotel room, knowing them again and again to obliterate time and terror of things converging. And for your knowledge of acquiescence, a new lesson. The sound from a street musician blowing blues trumpet reaches you through the open balcony door. When the rain comes down into the city you catch yourself on the first day, remembering. *Begin again.*

AUTOBIOGRAPHY

Born in early morning and starting to sink. There are some explanations; such a world. From the start, I melded through it, o so softly. Wanting to pass like rain, but I was recalled: voices, lights, clangorous noise. The sound the body makes in longing for sleep.

So what if it was a summer in season. What if the earth was green. The days were even then diminishing.

As you go, so shall you inherit the earth. Integration, though real, is temporary. It was too early to start thinking. Nevertheless. Such pointless need, but it does go that way. Escape, too, may be temporary, or hope can be held in slipping deliberation. At some point, darkness homes in. It was apparent there was much to be uneasy about. But finally warm. Finally safe.

Was listening. The air at dusk sounding with night birds and shivering. No worlds are separate. Succumb? Indeed, we can. It would be my way: I took this unto me. And for the time being, for the time what really happened was. This thing was a medium; I could silt my hands within it, softening sound and touch, mulling apprehension, covering what would be better to do without. I would never forget it. I would never forget the sensation of it.

I would not forget its sensation.

Tactile eminence shadowed over weeks of growing. Untoward light: pure shock. Stayed with me. Soft rambling step after rain in the dark, the moulding of foot to earth and hissing of terrible metal animals as they speed along their trails. Am I both separate and alone, I do pray. Find in me a reverent posture, but to whom this goes I would not venture. Softening medium steals the colour but I can summon it back again in superlative eminence. Go; now come. Particular, then, my rendered, silent bedlam?

> *The other clues: those who have passed on are more simply lovable. The word "shy" written in cement. Laughter, for nothing, and sleep, separated by periods of darkness. A small, sensual tragedy, for unlit stage. But played modestly, and with gravity.*

How many times must this happen. No worlds are separate, but I? I am. The dark was quiet. I could hear myself. In went even further in. Separate. Arrogant. Already hot with pride, and splendid. So. The limits of this body, always so warm and like silk, then nothing. The potential for resonance, at least.

At best. *The word "shy" written in cement.*

> *There is the other part. Mad for speed, for impact. Eros and maniacal. Haunted, where it's least predicted. The knowing silence of cats. Puzzling. Troubling. But how should it be managed? In goes much further than it seems. Less apparent: it could be useful. We may live as we are told, but our core in conflagration. At some point darkness comes homing in.*

The word of the mouth, how too infidelious, whose is this? Mine is a heavy tongue, unused to wielding. This was safety, at first. If I spoke, my silence would not be missed; but in silence myself could be within its own wiles, knowing by instinct ears are pierced only to hang rings from the flesh. *Within the flesh, myself, my core in conflagration.* Camouflage, quiet.

How can it matter? Listening can be learned optionally, and only in silence. Arduous for those initiated at birth; insuperable to those in other straits. The word of the mouth, set like to like, knowing its own. To whom this goes I would not venture. But soft you now—as poets say—I was no fit teacher for others.

In sleep the body lies very close to pleasure. Smoke, and mirrors. Leave it there where it's inclined. The first minutes upon waking: the heaviest and most desperate in time. Seems it to me. Sleep is a place to settle deep in alien conformations. The body was formed to resonate. To listen. How like my medium, my silent bedlam, yet find such stunning wants. I? A soprano in my dreams, but a contralto if I'm fortunate. And use that sussing voice to call the loving dead: Go; now come.

The loving dead in their particulars, subtly demanding, violently addictive. Malleable in their turn. Recalcitrant by nature. When I turn in sleep, it is to their overtures, knowing full well I will be undone for else. But find in me a reverent posture. When I lift my hands, the gesture carries. Their gratifications proffered, and endlessly protracted.

Amid the smoke, and mirrors.

I would not forget its sensation.

But for the time being, but for the time. I don't deny my errantness, but why should that be broadcast? I am a silent one—in all, what have I said of myself. There are some explanations. Mastered by love? Unlikely. Tip-turned in nature? Indeed. And what a task, explaining that, and for so little recompense.

Time be bothered in other mannered, expression, behooved content. Along and way. Those walks after rain in the dark did give me lessons. At some point, darkness will have its art.

Hanging rings from the flesh, those in other straits, and still they will not have silence. They will say "I don't know what you're saying, but I can't see it." They will say "Wouldn't you prefer someone you can love normally?" They will say "Put on the lights." "Put out the garbage." "Answer the phone."

Resource and tactile eminence. Certain gestures of hand are enough to reassure, and recall: no worlds are separate. It was like this, then that. I can live here, and still emerge there: now, it is bearable.

The limits of this body, my core, always so warm and like silk, made to resonate. Then yes. Contralto. Compose something in D minor, for voice, piano and cats. Those soft and silent ones, keeping time. Expression, behooved content.

*Conflagration in the drama
of the key. Who should know
this? Why should any. Is it
not a precious thing?*

Goeth before a fall. Separate, yes. Arrogant, yes. If I invent a fall to tell, it will be pleasing to some, and they may love me for it. Why should any. In reality, pride can be sustenance. In dreams, it is erotic. Sad, how many worlds have squandered themselves upon waking, but listen: the strain is still there. Making daylight randomly slung.

The time before a fall—entirely enticing. I am mad for smoke and mirrors, yes, I know. The real world, *such a term,* is not what we make it but what we can't avoid. So much, and so imperfect. I was no fit teacher for others *my core in conflagration* but my silence is some small payment for that. Camouflage. Quiet, where it's least expected. Am I not to be owed something in return?

In dreams, it is erotic. My composition, soft and silent, is thrilling. As is the voice to call the loving dead. Escape is temporary. Is necessary. I would know both darkness and its art. *Disquieted by that burning always.* My dear and rendered, silent bedlam, potent, buoyant, and randomly slung. That I was so much in command: what amazement. That I laid so much at the mercy: what a pleasure. In fact, my composition sounds like shades of water—glorious and brooding, blues and greys. And after the sun goes, the art of darkness.

As is well known.

Many fathoms below, dark and silent indeed. The loving dead, because they are there, and beautiful, and offer what is otherwise not to be had. Who shall blame me for such acceptance? Within my composition are many movements. Those limits, then nothing. That calm, then sleep. Apart from those in other straits, I spend much time there, set like to like. It is not real, *but such a world.*

> *Between loving dead and lapping worlds—there: it is bearable. And resonant. Summon the colour back again, what can be made of it, how temporary, how necessary. Daylight being what it is.*

Since I am so bold, I will say this much: where was it I could have gone had I not been recalled? *Go; now come.* Where to, in superlative eminence, do I send the colour, the loving dead? *Laughter is not always for nothing* no, not always, but from where does it arrive? Like my composition, it holds drama in its key—how kind of it, how discreetly compassionate. Perhaps *laughter, unprovoked,* but that would take some imagining: I do it every day, all the time, without warning *my core in conflagration*—why should any know that? How many times must this happen. *Discreet. Merciless.* The worlds that claim me are not always so, but always without end. Within the seething covenant, I do possess them too.

Think you not that there will be regrets? That such can be wholly triumphant, allowing no remorse and sadly abled? How can any be so tempered and not be seared? Soft you now. All is camouflage. Formed for resonance, yes, but it sounds perhaps different than expected. Less apparent. Darkness homes in, *silence being what it isn't,* knowing its own. *We shall call what we need.* Yes. *We shall keep what is precious.* Yes. Escape is momentary, *but superlatively eminent.*

I began by saying what of myself: not a story, surely, nor anecdote. There are some explanations, deep in alien conformation. Leave me there where I'm inclined. *It was regrettable* but always without end, untoward light, pure shock. Slipping deliberation. And how must it conclude, in sadness or singing power, modestly, and with gravity? The limits, then nothing. *But soft you now.* The days were even then diminishing.

OTHER ANVIL PRESS FICTION

BODY SPEAKING WORDS
Loree Harrell

MONDAY NIGHT MAN
Grant Buday

STOLEN VOICES/VACANT ROOMS
Steve Lundin/Mitch Parry

A CIRCLE OF BIRDS
Hayden Trenholm

STUPID CRIMES
Dennis E. Bolen